Solutions for COLD FEET

and other little problems

BY Carey Sookocheff

TUNDRA BOOKS

SOLUTIONS
FOR
A MISSING
SHOE

CHECK IN THE CLOSET

LOOK UNDER THE BED

SEARCH BEHIND THE COUCH

AND UNDER THE TABLE

WEAR A MISMATCHED PAIR

SOLUTIONS FOR GETTING CAUGHT IN THE RAIN

RUN

TAKE COVER OUTSIDE

SPLASH IN THE PUDDLES

SOLUTIONS FOR A MELTING ICE CREAM CONE

LOTS OF NAPKINS

EAT FAST

SHARE WITH A FRIEND

GET ANOTHER
ICE CREAM CONE

SOLUTIONS
FOR
A BORING DAY

FIND A FRIEND
TO PLAY WITH

SOLUTIONS FOR A FLYAWAY HAT

USE YOUR MITTENS

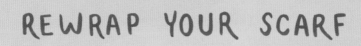

REWRAP YOUR SCARF

MAKE A SNOWMAN

SOLUTIONS

FOR

COLD FEET

BIG BOOTS

WARM SLIPPERS

A BLANKET

AND A DOG

For my dogs past and present who have warmed
both my feet and my heart.

Thank you to my editor, Tara, for seeing
potential in a postcard and for your huge help in making this
book happen. Thank you as well to my good friends Peggy
and Anne for helping me go from making pictures to
telling stories. And to my husband, Albert, thank you for
your encouragement, love and ice cream.

Library and Archives Canada Cataloguing in Publication

Sookocheff, Carey, 1972-, author, illustrator
     Solutions for cold feet and other little problems / written
     and illustrated by Carey Sookocheff.

Issued in print and electronic formats.
ISBN 978-1-77049-873-0 (bound).—ISBN 978-1-77049-874-7 (epub)

     I. Title.

PS8637.O56S65 2016   jC813'.6   C2015-905762-0
                                              C2015-905763-9

Published simultaneously in the United States of America by Tundra Books of
Northern New York, a division of Random House of Canada Limited, a Penguin
Random House Company

Library of Congress Control Number: 2015955124

Edited by Tara Walker
Designed by Carey Sookocheff
The artwork in this book was painted with acryl gouache
on watercolor paper and assembled digitally.
Printed and bound in China

www.penguinrandomhouse.ca

1 2 3 4 5   20 19 18 17 16

TUNDRA BOOKS | Penguin
Random
House